PUFFIN BOOKS

UK | USA | Canada | Ireland | Australia | India | New Zealand | South Africa

Puffin Books is part of the Penguin Random House group of companies whose
addresses can be found at global.penguinrandomhouse.com.

www.penguin.co.uk
www.puffin.co.uk
www.ladybird.co.uk

Penguin
Random House
UK

First published 2016

001

Text and illustrations copyright © FremantleMedia Limited, 2016
Danger Mouse is a trademark of FremantleMedia Limited. Licensed by
FremantleMedia Kids & Family Entertainment.
CBBC logo © BBC 2016
Written by Kay Woodward
Illustrations by Lea Wade

Set in Sabon MT Std 15/23

Printed in Great Britain by Clays Ltd, St Ives plc

A CIP catalogue record for this book is available from the British Library

ISBN: 978-0-141-36683-8

All correspondence to
Puffin Books
Penguin Random House Children's
80 Strand, London WC2R 0RL

ARE WE NEARLY THERE, YETI?

by Ernest Penfold

PUFFIN

The name's Penfold, Ernest Penfold.

I'm Danger Mouse's personal assistant and super sidekick and . . . drum roll . . . <u>**BFF**</u>!

What can I tell you about Danger Mouse? Well, firstly, he's the <u>greatest</u>. Secondly, he's <u>fantastic</u>. Thirdly, wherever there is **DANGER**, he'll be there. Which, fourthly, means that I'll be there too, because that's what sidekicks are for.

<u>Gulp.</u>

But the thing about super secret agents who think nothing of <u>parachuting into a volcano</u> or dangling off a cliff (before breakfast) is that they're usually too busy saving the world to write down how they do it. Though I can tell you that it's usually with some **BANGS** and **BOOMS** and an awful lot of **CRIKEYS** from me.

So let me introduce you to Danger Mouse's own personal reporter and biographer and storyteller . . . <u>ME!</u> (Did you guess? You did? Oh.)

I'm great at multitasking – did you know that I can escape from an evil genius **AND** eat an ice cream at the same time? So I'm the ideal person to write about Danger Mouse's terrifyingly exciting adventures. When I'm not too scared to look, that is.

Over and out,

CHAPTER ONE

'Oh, crikey,' I said. '*That* wasn't supposed to happen.'

I stared goggle-eyed at my *Giraffe Warriors* poster. Samurhino (the BEST *Giraffe Warriors* character) glared out from the picture at the drop of water that was running down from the drawing pin I'd ever-so-gently tapped into the wall of HQ to fix the poster there. A second drop chased after the first. Then a third. And after

that I sort of lost count because it wasn't
so much drops of water as an ACTUAL
WATERFALL. My Samurhino poster sprang
from the crumbling plaster to escape the
torrent and sailed away across the floor.

'Penfold?' called Squawkencluck. 'Any
idea why it's raining in my lab? You didn't
happen to burst a water pipe, did you . . . ?'

'Um . . . maybe!' I spluttered,
pressing both hands over the hole in the
wall, which was now as big as a dinner
plate. Oh, dear. Instead of stopping the
gushing water, this just made it spray in a
bazillion different directions.

'Hey, Penfold,' said Danger Mouse,
poking his head round the door. 'I was
wondering . . . is this another book in

our bestselling *Danger Mouse* adventure
series, starring me – Danger Mouse?'

I nodded. Water shot up my nose.

'Excellent!' Danger Mouse dived into a
yoga stretch before leaping to his feet for
a couple of star jumps so high he nearly
hit the ceiling. 'Better give the illustrator
an action shot then! So,' he went on,
raising a quizzical eyebrow, 'what's going

on here? I would offer to save you from terrible danger, but it looks as if all you need is some shower gel and a loofah!'

Danger Mouse thought his own joke was totally hilarious for the 1.21 seconds it took him to realize that, no, I hadn't created an indoor shower just to give the illustrator something really whizzy to draw and, no, I didn't know how to make it stop either. So then he stopped laughing and together we shouted, 'SQUAWKENCLUCK!' (in capitals, so HQ's resident science geek and all-round clever clogs would run faster).

'It's all very well saving the world every other week,' Squawkencluck said when she arrived, already dripping with water.

'But being able to survive on a day-to-day basis is pretty important too. I bet neither of you knows where the fuse box is either. And, no, it's NOT in the fridge.'

She turned a tiny tap under the sink and AT LAST the water stopped rinsing my eyeballs.

'Don't worry about that, Professor!' Danger Mouse said. 'Penfold and I are brilliant at surviving. We are ready for *anything*. Isn't that right, old chap?'

BANG! A gigantic explosion rocked HQ and all the lights went out.

'I say,' said Danger Mouse. 'Does anyone have a torch . . . ?'

Oh, blimey. It was only page six and already we had a major emergency

situation. And it was *all because of my
drawing pin*. Squawkencluck said it must
have pierced a water pipe, which flooded
HQ and – **BOOM!** – blew the electrics.
So now there was no water AND no power.

On the plus side, we did now have our
very own plunge pool downstairs.

By the next morning, I had proved beyond all reasonable doubt that 'Survival' was NOT my middle name. First, I'd dropped the last of the dry matches into the floodwater. Then the furniture I moved up to the top floor made the ceiling collapse. And then my brilliantly inventive idea for drying out the wet teabags by hanging them on the washing line turned out to be a total failure when they were pinched by pigeons.

'Blithering barnacles, Pigfold,' said Colonel K – or rather, his hologram did. It was far too dark and wet for him to appear in person. 'Can't you do anything useful?!'

'Yes!' I said proudly. 'I once made fourteen hundred cups of tea at a royal garden party. And my name is Penfold, sir.'

Colonel K shook his head. 'But can you

abseil down a rock face on a pair of braces? Can you live on worms for a week? Can you SURVIVE IN THE WILD?!'

'I survived a Boxing Day sale once,' I said. 'Does that count?'

'GERONIMO!' cried Danger Mouse, surfing towards me on a tea tray and sloshing to a halt.

Then he sank gracefully until he was knee-deep in water. 'Penfold, I've had a stupendous idea. You're not a survival expert simply because you've never been taught how to be one! So I'm going to fix that.'

I gulped. I might not be a survival expert, but I could sniff danger at a hundred paces and I was getting pretty huge whiffs right now.

'I'm going to take you on the trip of a lifetime . . . to the Himalayan mountains!' Danger Mouse went on. 'We'll live outdoors in the actual wild! We can hunt 'n' fish 'n' camp! Afterwards you'll be able to survive ANYTHING.'

'Can't we just go to a campsite at the

seaside and survive on fish and chips?' I asked hopefully.

'Nope!' said Danger Mouse, beaming from ear to ear. 'Not far enough away from civilization! And definitely not dangerous enough! Where we're going, you're going to need an exclamation mark at the end of *every sentence*!'

Oh, no, you're not.

Love, Penfold's editor

P.S. Mwah ha ha! (I've always wanted to say that.)

Oh, blimey. We hadn't even reached the end of Chapter One and already I was terrified. But Danger Mouse was raring to go.

'I'm raring to go!' he declared. (See, I told you.) He pressed the remote control for the Mark IV Danger Car. 'Come on, Penfold!'

'But, Chief,' I said, panic rushing through my veins like water from a burst, um, water pipe. 'Don't we need to pack? I know we need to survive in the wilderness, but even Arctic explorers take supplies with them. You know, tents, sleeping bags, whistling kettles, teabags, that sort of thing?'

'Good plan, Penfold!' said Danger Mouse. 'Grab everything we need – we leave in five minutes!'

FIVE MINUTES?! There wasn't even time to complain about how little time there was.

I sped around HQ grabbing essential items. One tent. One Danger-Mouse-shaped sleeping bag. One Penfold-shaped sleeping bag. That whistling kettle I mentioned. Five hundred teabags. Trekking poles. Hiking boots. Gaiters, which are apparently NOT swamp-dwelling reptiles – who knew? Helmets. A fishing net small enough to fit in my pocket. Two fancy headlamps with multicoloured beams that were invented by Squawkencluck for unexpected disco situations, but hey, they would do. One pocketknife with one hundred and seventy

blades (that didn't fit in my pocket).
Five hundred more tea bags. One ice axe.
Crampons (no, I had absolutely no idea
what those were either). Glacier glasses
(cooooool). I was determined not to forget
anything. Hats, gloves, thermal long johns,
camping stove, saucepans, tin mugs and
cereal bowls, inflatable sofa, cuddly toy...
I piled it all into the Mark IV. And then it
was time to go, and I hadn't even packed
the alarm clock – and did we have enough
tea bags? And *what about the toast rack*?!

'Yee-haw!' yelled Danger Mouse,
as the Mark IV roared upward into a
magnificent loop-the-loop.

I covered my mouth in horror. Reflected
in the wing mirror as we somersaulted in

the air, I saw the kettle, the helmets, the cuddly toy and nearly all the other essential items tumble out of the boot of the Mark IV and fall gracefully back to earth.

CHAPTER TWO

*B*adum-tsssssh!

'I say, Penfold,' said Danger Mouse.
'Did I tell a brilliant joke or something?
Wow. I'm hilarious without even trying!'

'Er, no,' I said. 'That was the sound
of us touching down with a saucepan
and an egg whisk hanging off the back of
the Mark IV. Apart from the tent, I think
that's just about all we have left of what

I packed, after your aerobatics. How will we survive in the Himalayas *now*, Chief?'

'Oops-a-daisy,' said Danger Mouse. 'Still, this means that we can survive properly, like real explorers, foraging for berries and fighting beasts with our bare hands. It'll be DANGEROUS.' He peered through the windscreen at a rippling lake, tipping his head right back to check out the mountains that vanished up and out of sight. 'Nice spot, isn't it? Not too touristy. Anyway, what are we having for tea? Pizza? I fancy a spinach one with an egg on top.'

'Chief,' I said, clambering out of the Mark IV, 'we're in the foothills of the Himalayas. I don't have a pizza oven with me. Or dough. Or spinach. Or an egg.

Although I do have some . . . JAM.' (Which, by the way, is my most favourite food ever.) I produced a jar out of my pocket, like a rabbit from a top hat. *'Ta-daaaaaa!'*

Things weren't looking so bad. We'd lived in the wild for six whole minutes and neither of us had been eaten by a Himalayan black bear or a Himalayan wild yak yet. Survival was EASY PEASY LEMON SQUEEZY –

All the lights went out.

'**HELP!**' I yelled, doing jazz hands, but faster. '**IT'S AN ATTACK OF THE KILLER BLUE SHEEP! PROBABLY! IT'S TOO DARK TO SEE THEM!**'

'What?!' I felt Danger Mouse leap into his ready-for-action Mouse Fu pose

beside me. 'Blue sheep?! It can't be.
We don't meet them till Book Seventeen.
Unless . . . Penfold, stop panicking. The
Himalayan mountains are getting in the
way of the setting sun! It's not an attack of
the killer blue sheep. It's just getting dark.'

'Getting DARK?' I quavered, thinking
longingly of the cuddly toy we dropped
over Turkmenistan. 'That's even worse
than killer blue sheep.'

A drumming noise began. It was
coming from somewhere in the direction
of Danger Mouse. Good heavens. This
was no time to record a backing track for
a drum-and-bass hit! By now, my eyes were
getting used to the darkness and I could
just see him. Danger Mouse wasn't riffing

on a set of drums, even though it sounded
like it. He was running on the spot.

'You might want to warn the illustrator
that there's A Really Whizzy Bit coming
up!' Danger Mouse panted. He ran faster.
His feet spun round, just as if he were
riding an invisible unicycle. Soon they
actually GLOWED. Now they were giving

off sparks! Faster and faster he sprinted.
I could see a circle of flickering light
where his feet whirred. It looked just like a
Catherine-wheel firework. And then –

Crackle.

The tiniest flame was flickering
beneath Danger Mouse's toes. Wow. He'd
started a real, true-life fire. In the wild.
WITHOUT A MATCH.

'Penfold, old chap,' said Danger
Mouse, 'sorry to interrupt you looking
on in amazement, but could you throw
me a few sticks of kindling to keep these
flames going?'

'Danger Mouse!' I cried. 'You're on
fire today!'

The world's greatest super secret agent

gave a small salute. 'Why, thank you.'

'No, you really ARE on fire,' I said, pointing. His feet were starting to smoke.

With a *BOING BOING BOING* and a *SPLASH*, Danger Mouse triple-jumped into the lake where his feet gave a long *HISSSS*.

'Ahhhhh,' he sighed. 'That's better. Your turn, Penfold. How would you like to try your hand at putting the tent up while I'm cooling down?'

'Sure!' I said. The orange glow of the campfire was making everything look, well, orange. It all felt a lot safer and cosier. I swaggered confidently over to the Mark IV and pulled out the random assortment of items that had survived the trip. Luckily, the tent was one of them. I shoved the rest in my pocket.

'Pitch it, Penfold!' called Danger Mouse.

'No problem!' I called back, and threw the tent as hard as I could. It flew straight into a Himalayan tree. Crikey. It was going to be difficult to sleep up there. Still,

Danger Mouse knew more about survival
than I did. Though it did seem odd that he
now had his head in his hands.

Crackle. Spit. Snap.

I could see the campfire burning
brightly through the canvas. Danger
Mouse had explained that pitching a
tent was quite different from pitching a
baseball. After untangling it from the
tree, he had demonstrated how to put
up our tiny triangular tent in just eighty-
seven easy moves. I was pretty sure that
I remembered about three of them. No,
two. Anyway, we were zipped up inside
and it was time to sleep. IN THE WILD.
(Did I mention we were in the wild?)

Meh-eh-eh-eh!

I jumped. 'What's that?'

'That's the Himalayan tahr,' said Danger Mouse sleepily. 'It's a type of . . . YAWN . . . wild mountain goat. Nothing to worry about.'

Rarrrrr!

'What's that?' I whispered.

'Just a snow leopard,' said Danger Mouse, closing his eyes. 'Friendly. I think.'

GRRR-OW-OW-OW-OW!

I sat bolt upright. 'And what is THAT?'

Danger Mouse opened his eyes. 'Hmm,' he said. 'That is not in my *Big Book of Himalayan Wildlife*.'

I gulped. On a scale of one to ten of scariness, this measured about one

million and three hundred thousand.
I closed my eyes and wished really
hard that I was somewhere else, doing
something less scary. Like base-jumping
from the Eiffel Tower or wrestling a
python or something. I opened them

again. No, I was still in the Himalayas.
And yet another peculiar noise was
coming from outside . . .

Thud . . . thud . . . thud . . . thud.

The thuds went round and round the
tent – slow, steady and totally terrifying.

'Do you mind if I shout *argh!* really
loudly?' I whispered to Danger Mouse,
who was pressing his ear to the canvas
and listening intently. (I knew things
were really bad, because I was too scared
even to make a joke about listening
intently IN A TENT.)

'Probably best not to,' he said. 'That
thing out there might eat you.'

Thud . . . thud . . . thud . . . TWANG!

Nooooooooo. That was the guy rope!

If it snapped, the tent would fall down and we would be Monster Midnight Snacks!

But even though the tent shuddered madly, the rope held and the circling footsteps went on, even louder now.

THUD ... THUD ... THUD ... THUD ... THUD ... THUD ... TWANGETTY-TWANG-DOINK ... **BOOM!** The tent wobbled. The ground shook like jelly. And then the most bloodcurdling sound of all tore through the night sky.

OWWWWWWWWW!

CHAPTER THREE

I listened hard, clenching my knees together to stop them knocking.

Outside, the most terrible thrashing and banging raged on. The tent swayed as if it were standing on the top of a mountain ridge in a force-eight gale.

'So can I shout *argh!* now?' I murmured in Danger Mouse's ear. I was quickly working my way through the thesaurus entry for *frightened*. I was already halfway between *panicky* and *petrified*.

'Afraid not,' he hissed back. 'My many years' experience of battling supervillains has taught me that when you've got a monster tangled in your guy ropes, don't embarrass them by startling them. They hate to look silly in front of an audience.'

I made a careful note of this and got on with being *scared stiff* and then *startled*.

There was one final *TWANG!* and the tent shuddered. The unseen being lumbered away, every footstep a minor earthquake. Finally, FINALLY, the commotion stopped.

'Right, show's over,' said Danger Mouse. 'Goodnight, Penfold!'

'Chief . . . ?' I said. The ground might

have stopped shaking, but I hadn't.
'Aren't you going to catch the monster
and truss it up in ropes and tie it to a
tree? What if it comes back in the night?
What will we dooooooo?'

Danger Mouse snored in reply.

Oh, blimey. We were alone in the
foothills of the Himalayas, a wild creature
was stalking us and Danger Mouse was
ASLEEP. Humph. I would never be able to
drop off. Not in a million yearszzzz . . .

'Wakey-wakey!' cried Danger Mouse,
zooming past the open tent flap. He ran
up the nearest tree, did a neat backflip
and landed like a gymnast, before diving –
SPLOOSH! – into the lake.

We hadn't been eaten! YAY. Giddy
with relief, I climbed out of the tent and
stepped carefully over the footprints.

Ahem. Sorry. S-l-o-w d-o-w-n. Let's
hold it right there. Now, REWIND.

Footprints.

Big footprints.

No, monster-sized footprints.

'DANGER MOUSE!' I shouted, because I knew beyond a doubt what had been circling our tent last night. And now . . . terror held me in its iron fist. 'ARRRRRGGGGGGHHHHHH!' I yelled. It was an extra-specially looooong and LOUD *argh!* to make up for the all those that I missed out on yelling last night. 'I've found footprints and I think they belong to . . . A YETI!'

Danger Mouse splashed his way out of the lake. 'A whati?'

'A yeti!' I repeated. 'An Abominable Snowman!'

'Blimey, both of them?'

'Noooooooo,' I said. 'They're the *same thing.*'

'Aha!' said Danger Mouse, who had activated his EyePatch and was now busy searching the internet. He spun through different images, pausing when he found a picture of a hairy, apelike creature with enormous feet trudging along a snowy mountain ridge. 'Is this what you mean, Penfold?'

I trembled. 'Yes, Chief.'

'*Even though stories and sightings of the yeti date back to ancient times*,' Danger Mouse read, '*the yeti's existence has never been proven. But, ever hopeful of finding a brand-new species, experts and explorers search for it still. One day, they hope to find the creature nicknamed the Abominable Snowman –*' he paused dramatically – '*SOMEWHERE IN THE HIMALAYAS.*'

'Somewhere like here?' I said shakily, and pointed with a wobbly finger at the words scrawled on the side of our tent.

I'M COMING TO GET YOU, DANGER MOUSE! (AND YOU TOO, PENFOLD.)

BE SCARED. BE VERY SCARED.

'Well, that's a turn-up for the books,' said Danger Mouse. 'It doesn't say on the internet that yetis can write. Very neat. The grammar's not bad either.'

'ARGH!' I said, again. 'I WANT TO GO HOME.'

'Home?' Danger Mouse looked at me as if I'd just suggested that he stop being a super secret agent and become a full-time knitter instead. 'I was kidding, Penfold,' he said, taking down the tent, folding it with whizzy origami skills and popping it back into its bag in twelve seconds flat. 'Even if yetis did exist, I'm pretty sure they wouldn't be able to write. Besides, I'm almost positive that silly warning was already on the tent when we put it up. It must have been written there when we last went camping in, um, 1992.'

'Are you sure . . . ?' I said.

'Over eighty-two per cent certain,' said Danger Mouse confidently. 'There are no such things as yetis, Penfold. We're simply being trailed by an ordinary hungry wild animal. Nothing to worry about.'

'And it won't eat us?' I said, still a little unsure about this.

'It might try!' said Danger Mouse, limbering up. 'Ahh, a nice dangerous wild animal. What a relief, Penfold. I thought we were just going to be dangling off precipices and eating worms for a week. *Boring.*'

He headed off in the direction of the nearest slope, the tent bag balanced on

his shoulder and the rope hanging like
a chunky garland round his neck. 'Let's
get trekking, Penfold,' he called back to
me. 'I haven't taught you how to make a
bivouac yet – that's a kind of shelter,

you know. I've not taught you how to
tie the six hundred and twenty-three
different knots in my repertoire yet either.
And it won't be a survival trip if we don't
sleep on a rock face at least once!'

I hardly heard him. I was too busy
staring at one of the trees behind Danger
Mouse's ears. There, between long,
silvery green leaves, I was almost certain
I could see a pair of eyes watching us.
Did they belong to the wild animal that
had circled our tent last night? I tried to
remember what Danger Mouse had said,
but I couldn't help thinking that they did
look a bit . . . yeti-ish.

Then I blinked . . . and the eyes were
gone.

CHAPTER FOUR

Danger Mouse marched up the mountain with me hot on his heels. And I mean HOT. I was puffing like a steam train. I was panting like a pair of pants. This mountain-climbing lark was officially Very Hard Work. How did real mountain-climbers *do* this, carrying those massive rucksacks? Perhaps it was a good thing that our survival gear had tumbled into oblivion. This would have been

super difficult while carrying a toast rack.
(Mmm . . . Toast.)

'Chief,' I gasped, 'can we stop for a
snack now?'

'We've only been walking for seventeen
minutes,' said Danger Mouse. 'Keep
going, Penfold. Onward and upward!'

Wearily, I trudged after him. We
skirted the lake, dodging the car-sized
boulders that littered our route. Then we
headed for the wood beyond. Yikes. It
was dark and sinister in here. Yeti-shaped
shadows loomed spookily between
the trees, one minute towering over us,
the next leering under low branches.
Leaves rustled as if blown by an invisible
wind – which is why we didn't hear the

craaaaaaack! above us until it was almost too late.

Oh, crikey! A branch as big as a baboon's arm was slowly tearing itself away from a tree trunk, RIGHT ABOVE US.

'*Help!*' I whispered, because my voice had gone on strike.

'. . . and the best way to avoid mosquito bites altogether,' Danger Mouse was saying, 'is to rub yourself all over with rosemary, sage, peppermint and garlic. Why are you poking me, Penfold? And why are you pointing up? OH.' He dropped the tent with a *THUNK*. He climbed up the tree trunk at lightning speed. And then he launched himself at the teetering branch, kicking it with a *KERPOW*.

It arced away from me and fell to the ground. *CRASH!* Danger Mouse landed softly beside it, bending his knees in a perfect ballerina's plié to absorb the impact.

'Th-thank you,' I stammered.

'Isn't surviving FUN?' Danger Mouse said, as he picked the tent up again and hopped over the fallen branch. 'Although I wonder which way is north? I do hope we don't get lost in here.'

Lost? In a wood full of death-trap branches? I didn't fancy that AT ALL. I stumbled after Danger Mouse, clambering over a fallen tree trunk and – *oops!* – slithering down the other side, which was covered in slippery moss.

'Wow. You're a natural, Penfold!'

Danger Mouse clapped me on the back. 'You didn't tell me that you knew to look for the moss that grows on the shady northern side of trees. You're better than a compass!'

'Er . . . that's right, Chief,' I said, distracted by two lights glinting between the trees just behind us. They looked extraordinarily like the whites of a yeti's eyes, blinking slowly at me. Oh, heck.

To tell Danger Mouse or not to tell
Danger Mouse? I decided not to. After
all, I'd just won a few survival-skills
points for finding north. I didn't want to
lose them all again by sounding silly. It
was probably just a trick of the light.

'Let's go!' declared Danger Mouse.

I didn't need telling twice.

Pfffft. Somehow I'd been walking for 137
hours and yet it was *still the same day*.

'See these tiny shadows?' Danger Mouse
asked, pointing to the shade beneath a
cluster of mountain flowers. 'These show us
that the sun is almost directly overhead. It's
the middle of the day. It's time to fish in the
mountain streams for our lunch!'

'Pardon?' I was much too busy keeping an eye on a looming, mossy boulder to pay attention. Was that some fur sticking out round the side of it? Oh, blimey. The yeti was following us! It was lying in wait, and when we least expected it, it would leap out and gobble us up! No one would ever know that we had been eaten by the world's scariest undiscovered creature.

And then who would live at the Danger
Agency's HQ and use Squawkencluck's
gadgets and save the world from Baron
Greenback and . . . 'LUNCH?' I echoed,
finally clocking what Danger Mouse had
said. 'Yes, *please.*'

'Roger that,' said Danger Mouse. He
activated the EyePatch. 'Just let me do a
spot of research into fishing. How exciting.
Now, how do we catch the breadcrumbed
sort? And I wonder how easy it is to rustle
up some chips at altitude . . . ?'

While Danger Mouse was busy scouring
the internet, I kept a close eye on the
suspicious boulder. But there was no longer
a tuft of fur in sight. Not a wisp. Not a
strand. Hmm. It must be the altitude,

messing with my mind. I'd start imagining beds with thick mattresses and duck-down duvets soon. Oh, I *did* hope so.

'Hook, line, sinker . . . Got it,' said Danger Mouse, deftly moving virtual screens to and fro. He paused to read a message from HQ.

Greetings, survivors! it said. *Fancy deciding to combine a survival course with a trip to the top of Everest. Bravo! Good show! Are you nearly there yet? Toodle-pip! Colonel K.*

'DANGER MOUSE?' I wailed.

'Well, it seemed a shame to come all this way and not take a stroll up Everest too,' he said, looking bashful. 'It's not like we have a deadly villain to outwit, is it? And Everest is just an itty-bitty little mountain . . .'

'But what about the yet— I mean . . .
the wild animal?' I spluttered. 'What if it
eats us?'

'Pah! I'd like to see it try!' Danger
Mouse announced. 'Now, this fishing lark
seems a bit of a faff, so how about we
feast on some figs instead . . . ?'

The day wore on. There were no further
sightings of watchful eyes or suspicious
tufts of hair and there was barely anything
really dangerous going on (unless you
count the boulder as big as Berkshire that
tumbled down the mountainside and
missed us by millimetres, or the trickling
stream that turned into a torrent once we'd

paddled halfway across it). I began to relax
a little. As Danger Mouse said, this was
the Great Outdoors and nail-biting stuff
happened all the time. It didn't necessarily
mean we were being stalked by a yeti.

And it wasn't as if we'd been squashed or washed away or anything, was it?

So that was good.

'Er . . . Chief?' I said, as we were huddled round Danger Mouse's instant campfire that evening, 'I've had an idea. How about we set a trap for your, um, wild animal?'

'Brilliant!' Danger Mouse replied. His eyes sparkled with glee. 'So, let's build a replica of Big Ben and hang a rope from the minute hand. Then using a detachable pulley, we can attach a supersized lobster pot to the end of the rope. Just before midnight, we put a completely deeeeeelicious Sunday roast on a plate directly under the lobster pot. Our totally

dangerous wild animal won't be able to resist. When the clock strikes twelve, the pulley releases, the lobster pot plummets and *the wild animal is captured*!'

'Or we could just dig a big hole, carefully place some big leaves over it and wait until the wild animal falls in,' I said. 'Or is that too obvious?'

'Hmm.' Danger Mouse considered this for a moment before declaring, 'Penfold, I like your style. Let's do it!'

So that's what we did. And then we huddled inside the tent, where, even though I tried not to sound scared, my teeth chattered like a pair of maracas. At first, everything was dead quiet. Then, just like the night before, heavy footsteps started padding around outside the tent.

Thud ... thud ... thud ... thud ... thud.

Then slowly, slowly, ever so slowly, the tent door began to unzip.

Editor's note

There will now be a brief intermission to give readers time to finish any overdue homework or eat their vegetables or practise the violin or do any of the other trillion things that grown-ups are always nagging them to do.

ONLY JOKING.

On with the book!

CHAPTER FIVE

D id someone press fast forward? In a flash, the tent flaps were pulled aside and a huuuuuuuge head burst through the doorway, almost filling the space. Danger Mouse and I shrank back. The enormous monster stared at us, its indigo eyes blinking slowly in the gloom. It looked as if it were trying to decide whether we'd taste better accompanied by mixed veg or buttery mash. Its head bristled with thick, shiny fur that seemed to reflect the colours around it – the perfect camouflage. And when its mouth opened wide, I could see rows of huge teeth inside, as long and as sharp as kitchen knives. Oh, crumbs. We really were for the chop this time!

'I say,' growled a voice so deep it made the Pacific Ocean look like a paddling pool. 'I saw you eating jam earlier. Do you have any left? I love jam.'

Danger Mouse blew out a sigh of relief that ruffled the creature's fur. Then he flexed his muscles quickly. 'Just for the record,' he said, 'I wasn't scared. Just out of breath.' He raised an eyebrow. 'If you don't mind me asking, what *are* you, exactly?'

'I'm a yeti,' said the yeti.

'Well, I never,' said Danger Mouse. 'You do exist, after all.'

I whooped loudly and did a quick tap dance to celebrate. 'I was right! It's a real, true-life yeti and we found it! And, oh my goodness, we're alone in the Himalayas with a real, true-life yeti and WHAT IF IT EATS US?' I stopped doing the shuffle-hop step and looked around for escape routes. The yeti was taking up all the room. There was no way out!

The yeti rolled its eyes. 'Of course I'm not going to eat you,' it said. 'I'm vegetarian. I only wanted some jam.'

I reached into the inside pocket of my suit. 'Do you like blackcurrant jam?' I whispered.

'I don't like it,' rumbled the yeti.

I gulped.

'I *love* it.'

The yeti opened its massive jaws and bared its teeth. Uh-oh. It had changed its mind about being vegetarian and now

IT WAS GOING TO EAT US AFTER
ALL. Er, hang on. That's unless the
weird, scary grimace on its face actually
meant that the yeti was *smiling . . . ?*

Wow. It *was*. Shock of the century!
The yeti truly didn't want to eat us. It
didn't even want to chase us helter-skelter
down the mountainside for a laugh.
Instead, the Himalayas' star mystery
attraction was properly NICE. He was
also terribly polite and super kind and
went by the name of Julian. He didn't
even mind that we'd tripped him up with
our wild-animal trap. (Turns out we'd
made it way too small for a yeti. Yetis
are BIG. He made our giant hole in the
ground look like a teeny-tiny pothole.)

Julian the yeti survived in the Himalayas
by hiding from predators with his special
camouflage fur, and living on explorers'
food that he whipped out of their tents.

'I know that stealing is bad and wrong,' the yeti said sorrowfully, 'but look at it from my point of view. If I even set foot in a supermarket to buy bread and jam and things, imagine the fuss. I'd be swamped with scientists and journalists. And then my face would be plastered all over the newspapers and I'd never get a minute's peace. I'm a shy sort of chap. I'm not good with crowds.'

'So if all you wanted was jam, why did you try to scare us by stamping round and round the tent last night and tonight?' asked Danger Mouse.

Julian stared at us, a sticky pawful of jam halfway to his mouth. 'But I thought you knew,' he said.

'Knew what?' asked Danger Mouse, narrowing his eyes. He sprang to his feet and raised his arms in his ready-to-receive-surprising-information pose.

'I was staying close to your tent,' said Julian, 'because I was scared of the villain terrorizing the Himalayas.'

'The villain terrorizing the Himalayas?' Danger Mouse repeated.

'That's who wrote the warning message on your tent,' explained Julian. 'And the scoundrel must have been *really* fast, because I didn't even see them do it. One minute, no message, and then I turned back round and there it was!' He chuckled. 'You didn't think *I* wrote it, did you? I'm a yeti. I can't write.'

'Result!' cried Danger Mouse. 'You know what this means, don't you? Two villains in one book!'

Julian coughed politely. 'Technically, I'm not actually a villain,' he said.

'Excuse me,' I interrupted. 'We seem to be a little off topic here. It's GREAT that Julian isn't going to eat us for breakfast, but has everyone forgotten we're still being tracked by a totally scary and probably dangerous *real* enemy? Can we focus, please?'

'Ah, yes,' said Danger Mouse. 'Concentrate, everyone.'

So I looked at Danger Mouse. Danger Mouse looked at Julian. Julian looked at me. I looked back at Julian. Julian looked

back at me. We both looked at Danger
Mouse. And then Danger Mouse voiced
the question that was pinging backwards
and forward between us like an out-of-
control table football.

'So if you didn't write the message,
Julian,' said
Danger Mouse,
who did?'

CHAPTER SIX

The next day dawned at the usual time of Very Early. The sky was pink. Tattered charcoal clouds hung above the jagged mountaintops like dirty washing. A cold wind blew.

'*Ta-daaaaaa!*' yelled Danger Mouse. He kickboxed his way out of the tent (which was a shame, because it meant there was now a breezy Danger-Mouse-shaped hole in the side of it).

I squeezed out after him, clambering over Julian, who was so deeply asleep that he didn't even stir when I accidentally sat on his head. So I whispered 'JAM' in his ear, which woke him at once.

'Look sharp, Penfold,' said Danger Mouse. 'Our villain may not have been stomping round the tent last night, but they're out there somewhere! Let's check for footprints . . .'

'No need to check for those, dear boy,' said Julian. 'I was so jolly cross about your mystery enemy making me look bad that I kept watch all night long. I only just got into bed when you got up! And I can say with absolute certainty that NO ONE went anywhere near your tent.'

'Then what's *that* . . . ?' said Danger Mouse, pointing to the side of the tent. Below our mysterious enemy's original message, there was a brand-spanking-new one:

I'M NOT KIDDING, YOU KNOW.

I'M OUT TO GET YOU, DANGER MOUSE.

(AND YOU TOO, PENFOLD.)

Oh, no. I gulped so hard, it felt like swallowing a football. Who was out to get us? And why didn't they just show themselves?!

Julian the yeti hung his head. 'I'm so terribly sorry,' he said. 'I wanted to protect you and I've failed. No one's ever going to believe that I'm really a good guy. I will be labelled "the Terror of the Himalayas" FOR EVER.'

'Don't worry,' said Danger Mouse. He began to limber up, stretching his arm muscles and touching his toes. 'We believe you! Even if, um, nobody else does. Anyway, relax! You can leave it to the professionals now. Together, Penfold and I will solve this mystery and rid the Himalayas of evil!'

'Does this mean you're cancelling the survival-skills course, Danger Mouse?' I asked hopefully. 'We can't really fight evil *and* learn how to make a bivouac, can we? We won't have time.'

Danger Mouse jogged round the camp, swinging his arms in big circles before hanging from the branch of a nearby tree, where he did a couple of hundred high-speed pull-ups. 'Of course not,' he said, springing upright after a burpee (apparently this is a fiendishly hard exercise move and not a funky belch). 'We can do *both*!'

'In that case, you might have to demonstrate how to build a bivouac sooner than you think,' I said with a shiver.

'Why?' Danger Mouse looked puzzled.
'Because the tent's just disappeared.'

We looked back at where the tent had stood. Now there was just an expanse of bare earth. Some real-life tumbleweed rolled by, just to hammer home the fact that there really was absolutely nothing there.

The fear factor stepped up another gear. Someone was watching us. Someone was following us. Someone was stealing our stuff. And whoever it was, they were close by. It was like being haunted, but without a ghost giving us occasional clues and *whoo-ha-has* to point us in the right direction.

But Danger Mouse was hopping with excitement. 'Come on,' he said. 'I'm not having this scaredy-cat bad guy ruining our plans! We can hunt them down and we can capture them AND we can reach the top of Everest in record time. The villain seems intent on following us, so let's lead them up the mountain path where there's nowhere for them to hide! Then I can use my devilishly clever plan to trap and defeat them.'

PHEW. It was Danger Mouse to the rescue! He'd save the day again! And we were only on page seventy-five. Oooh. Did this mean we could spend the last four chapters relaxing at HQ with a cup of tea?

'How?' I said, flooded with relief. 'What's your plan?'

'That's the devilishly clever bit,' said Danger Mouse. 'I haven't thought of it yet!

So our enemy will NEVER be able to guess it. Meanwhile, we will have the element of surprise!'

'Oh, crumbs,' I said. That wasn't *quite* the reply I was hoping for.

We set off. Danger Mouse marched ahead. I scurried along behind, trying not to trip over my own feet with terror. Julian brought up the rear, keeping watch for any enemies on our tail. I didn't fancy his chances. He hadn't scored highly on the Spotting Intruders Index so far.

Up we went. Up, up, up. The trees were thinning out now, the ground brownish, barren and bare. And then we were above the treeline. From now on, all we had to look forward to was rock. And not the musical sort.

Abruptly, Danger Mouse skidded to a halt. *Screech!* I bumped into him. *Doink!* Julian the yeti bumped into me. *DOINK!* We were all squeeeeeezed together in the Himalayas' most ridiculous sandwich. (Mmm . . . A sandwich.)

'What's up, Danger Mouse?' I asked. 'Are we stopping for a snack?'

'Take a look, Penfold,' said the world's greatest super secret agent, hopping neatly to one side.

I leaned forward and then gasped as the ground fell away beneath me, tumbling into a crevasse so deep the bottom was out of sight. The edge of the crevasse looked shiny and new, as if the mountain had only just been blasted open. I felt nervous all over again. Someone really was out to get us!

'Isn't this *splendid*?' said Danger Mouse, totally unfazed. 'Now we can practise our rope skills! What we're going to do here is build a rope bridge and then we'll whizz across to the other side in a trice. It's almost too easy. I might walk across on my hands to make it more death-defying.'

'I'm not frightfully good with heights,' muttered Julian.

'Chief?' I squeaked. 'Can I have a piggyback . . . ?'

'You'll both be FINE,' said Danger Mouse, unhooking the rope from round his neck and quickly tying a lasso at one end. He hurled it into the far distance. With pinpoint accuracy the circle of rope fell over a tree stump. Hurray! Danger Mouse whooped and punched the air, before looping the other end of the rope round a handy rock on our side of the crevasse. And then he dived into action, zooming back and forth over the wide, deep, gaping HOLE OF DOOM to knot us a bridge of champions. Before I had

time to lose my nerve, Danger Mouse had scooted across, tugging me after him. We looked back at the far side of the crevasse. Where was Julian? Had he fallen in and tumbled right down to Australia?!

'I hope you don't mind,' said Julian, who
– as if by magic – was now standing beside
us, his fur shining so brightly in the sun that
I was blinded for a second. 'I walked round
the edge instead.'

Aw, shucks. The crevasse was only
about thirty metres wide. There was no
need for the complicated bridge. I was so
surprised that I let go of the rope Danger
Mouse had just hauled back and handed
to me for safekeeping. The whole thing
slithered over the edge of the crevasse and
tumbled out of sight.

You know how I mentioned we had
only one piece of kit left?

Make that no pieces of kit left.

Gulp.

The sun vanished behind a purplish
cloud and an icy gust of wind blew across
the mountainside. *Brrrr*. I hadn't been
this cold since I'd accidentally fallen into
the freezer at the supermarket when I was
searching for the longest sell-by dates.
Nervously, I looked all around. Once again,
I had the oddest feeling we were being
watched. Where *was* this terrifying villain?

But everything was still, apart from a
herd of mountain goats in the distance.
How pretty! Oooh, they were coming
closer, gambolling along as if they were
in an advert for charming chalet holidays.
Awww. They were quite a bit closer
now. I could see their hooves kicking up

dirt as they ran. Oh. Were they running towards us? Um . . . no. They were STAMPEDING towards us.

'DANGER MOUSE! JULIAN!' I shouted. 'RUN!'

CHAPTER SEVEN

'A race!' shouted Danger Mouse. 'Oh, goody! I do hope it's hurdles.'

With a burst of speed that made the Mark IV look slow, we were soon sprinting up the mountainside. In fact, we were going so quickly the illustrator couldn't draw the scenery fast enough, which was GREAT because when you're running up a blank page, there are no trip hazards or *anything*.

'My word, Penfold,' said Danger

Mouse, not even a tiny bit out of breath,
'I haven't travelled this fast since I was last
shot out of a cannon.'

Bzzzzzzzt!

'I say, DM,' said Colonel K's hologram,
joining us as we ran. 'I just dropped by to
ask if you chaps needed any vital supplies
or fancied a takeaway, because I'm pretty
sure there's a pizza place in Willesden
Green that delivers. But you seem to be
having such tremendous fun that I'll let you
get on with it. Byeeeee!'

'STOP, Colonel!' I panted. 'Help! Save
us! Yes, please. I'll have a Hawaiian with
extra cheese!' But he was gone.

Five thousand metres further uphill,
we'd lost the supersonic goats, the

illustrator had caught up with us and
sketched us a background, and Danger
Mouse had won gold. We were now *much*
higher up in the Himalayas.

Small drifts of snow dotted the mountainside. There was an excellent view of Everest from here. Hmm. It looked quite steep. I hoped there was a cable car. Or at least an escalator. And there'd better be a gift shop at the summit. There was no way I was climbing to the top of the world and going home without a fridge magnet.

'Someone spooked those goats,' I puffed. 'Someone left us those warning messages! Someone stole our tent and ripped a hole in the mountainside! Someone's out to get us, Danger Mouse!'

'Yes, yes,' said Danger Mouse, who was still looking disappointed that nobody had given him an actual gold medal. He stroked his chin. 'But who

could it *be*? And how have they managed
to sneak past us so many times?'

'Well, don't look at me,' said Julian
huffily. 'I was with you the whole time.
I'm the good guy, remember?'

'I wasn't looking at you,' said Danger
Mouse. 'I was staring into the middle
distance like they do on TV detective
dramas.' He jumped to his feet. 'Anyway, we
haven't got time to stop and chat. Mount
Everest is waiting for us! And a villain with
no face and a nearly vertical mountain path
are NOT reasons to stop climbing now.
Plus, I still haven't taught you how to scale a
rock face using just your fingernails.'

'But what if the mystery villain strikes
again?' I said.

Danger Mouse grinned. 'So far today we've survived a terrible tent theft, a certain-death crevasse crossing and a herd of stampeding goats. A fiendish attack will round the day off nicely!'

'Yay,' I said.

'Er, terribly sorry to interrupt,' said Julian, 'but my yeti senses tell me that we're about to be hit by an . . .'

'Apple pie with custard?' I said hopefully. 'Almond tart? Assortment of soft-centred chocolates?'

There was a sudden, terrifying, thunderous roar that sounded horribly like an express train approaching. Except it wasn't a train. It wasn't even my stomach grumbling. It was something much, much scarier than that.

'. . . *avalanche*!' finished Julian.

I stared up at the approaching disaster, my eyes goggling. High above us, the snow was moving, slowly at first, then with gathering speed. The avalanche gobbled everything in its path. It uprooted trees. It carried along giant boulders as easily as if they were marshmallows. I stared upward, mesmerized. The wave of destruction was about to sweep us down into the valley below.

We didn't stand a chance. Any second now, we would be TOAST.

Whoooooosh!

Relax, Danger fans! Take it easy. That wasn't the snow whisking us away on a tide of destruction. Well, I mean, it sort of was. But, before we got whisked, Danger Mouse reached out one arm for a tree branch flying by and the other for me and Julian. He hopped on to the tree branch as if it were a snowboard, and dragged us after him.

WHOOOOOOSH! We sailed down the tide of snow on the back of the branch. *BUMP!* We soared up into the air, flying off the top of a boulder (it was never going to be a smooth ride with

Danger Mouse steering). *Crrrrrunch!*
We slid to a standstill at the end of the
avalanche. I slipped sideways off the
branch, basically frozen solid with fear.

Danger Mouse, on the other hand,
leaped up and took an enormous running
jump off the end of the branch on to
solid ground. 'That was fun! Now it's
bivouac time!' he declared.

Blimey. How did he ALWAYS have so
much energy?!

While I worked on regaining the
feeling in my fear-frozen limbs and Julian
shook the snow and debris from his
shining fur, the world's greatest super
secret agent began building a bivouac.
He ran back and forth at lightning speed,

gathering logs and leaves and moss and piling them artistically on top of each other. I had to admit that not only was he brilliant at saving the world, Danger Mouse was pretty good at constructing survival shelters too.

'So . . . ?' he said, thirty minutes later. 'What do you think of it?'

I stood well back so that I could take it all in. Wow. Danger Mouse's bivouac had three storeys, two staircases (one spiral) and a large atrium featuring a model of Danger Mouse himself – all made from branches and leaves. Oh, and a turret. And an ornamental garden. And fountains. And a shed. With a lawnmower in it.

'You don't think it's a little much for an overnight stay?' I said cautiously.

'Not a bit of it!' said Danger Mouse. 'This will show our mysterious enemy that we're a force to be reckoned with! They won't DARE to attack us inside *this*.'

'Danger Mouse,' I whispered nervously, 'please don't go saying things like that. Something awful always happens when you say nothing can go wrong.'

'Not this time, Penfold!' said Danger Mouse.

FLASH!

A bright blue ball of light exploded out of nowhere and sped towards the bivouac. It landed at the entrance with a small *phut*. For a moment, nothing at all happened.

Then with the tiniest rustle, a single leaf
tottered and fell, and then . . . the entire
bivouac crumpled like a house of cards.

'*Ha ha ha haaaaaa!*'

'I don't think this is very funny,
Penfold,' said Danger Mouse. 'I loved
that bivouac. I was going to enter it into
this year's Best Bivouac Competition.'

I swallowed. 'I'm not laughing, Chief.'

'Then it's not funny, *Julian*,' said
Danger Mouse.

'I'm not laughing either,' said the yeti.
'I thought it was you.'

'Chief . . . ?' I said.

'Go ahead, Penfold,' said Danger
Mouse.

'*ARRRRRRGHHHHHHHHH!*'

CHAPTER EIGHT

'Finished?' asked Danger Mouse.

'Not quite, Chief,' I said. 'ARGHHHHH! Yes, that's about it.'

'Excellent,' said Danger Mouse. 'Now, where were we?'

I folded my arms in my best businesslike manner. 'Well,' I said. 'We're just at the beginning of Chapter Eight, which means we've got to unmask the mysterious villain who fired that blue ball of light pretty soon or something really bad will happen.'

'What's *that?*' said Julian.

'We'll run out of pages,' I replied.

'*Ha ha ha haaaaaa!*'

The nasty laugh echoed right in my ear and I shot into the air with fright. Crikey. I didn't think I'd been *that* funny. Or maybe I had. Oooh. Perhaps I could get a part-time job as a comedian and then I wouldn't have to do battle with danger every da– OUCH. Something *poked* me. Hard. Oh, my giddy aunt. *There was something there.*

'*Help!*' I cried – or I would have done if my voice hadn't chosen right then to go on holiday.

Desperately, I looked for Danger Mouse and the yeti. They were a short distance away, scouring the mountainside for clues. I waved my arms frantically.

'Yoo-hoo!' called Julian, waving back. Then he got on with staring down into the valley and then up at Everest. He must have been looking for the strange blue flash that had destroyed Danger Mouse's prize bivouac. He needn't have bothered. The mystery villain wasn't up or down. THEY WERE RIGHT HERE.

'Help!' I mouthed at Danger Mouse. But he was too busy levering up massive rocks with his little finger and didn't see me either.

I took a deeeeeep breath. I had to stay calm. Of *course* I wasn't being poked. That was completely ridiculous. It must be the lack of tea. That was it. My brain was starved of tea and I was starting

to imagine things . . . But then something
yanked my tie. Hard. I definitely felt that.

And I heard a little snigger too. Just a
nasty little laugh, right behind me.

Suddenly, I had it.

'Danger Mouse!' I cried. Hurray!
My voice was back. 'I think the villain is
INVISIBLE. That's why haven't been able
to spot them!'

I batted my hands around me frantically.
The villain was right here! Poking me and
yanking my tie! But my hands didn't hit
anything. Blast it. The invisible villain must
have slipped off again.

'By Jiminy, you're right!' said Danger
Mouse, who was now balancing at
the edge of a precipice on his tiptoes.

'Penfold, you're a genius! That'll explain why the mystery villain is nowhere to be found on the mountainside and why there's no sign of them at the bottom of this enormous drop.'

'Er, Danger Mouse . . . ?' I said nervously. 'I wouldn't stand there if I were you.'

'Don't panic, Penfold!' called Danger Mouse. 'Danger's my middle name! Well, actually, it's my first name. But you know what I mean. ANYWAY, I'd like to offer you my personal guarantee that I won't fall into oblivion – Ooops!'

I watched in horror as Danger Mouse jolted forward and plummeted out of sight. He didn't have a parachute! (It fell out of the Mark IV over Romania.) I ran towards

the spot where he'd vanished and looked
down the nearly vertical slope on the
other side. There was no sign of Danger
Mouse. None at all. Not even a speech
bubble with a 'YEE-HAH!' inside it.
Nooooooo. He was gone for ever!!

'Sorry to interrupt,' said a familiar
voice, 'but would you mind *not* standing
on my fingers? It makes it rather difficult
to cling on to this crumbling precipice,
you know.'

'Danger Mouse!' I cried, stepping
back on to the mountainside and hugging
him tightly when he jumped up, before
letting go with a polite *ahem*. 'I didn't see
you down there!'

'Clearly,' said Danger Mouse, blowing

on his fingertips. 'But here I am and all's well, despite our invisible villain's attempt to push me off the edge. Well done for working out the old invisibility thing, Penfold. You're a genius!'

'Thanks awfully, Chief,' I said, and I began to glow with pride, but then I suddenly got too anxious for that.

Something was worrying me even more than the fact we were being targeted by an invisible enemy with a nasty laugh, halfway up the Himalayas and approximately 8,487.25763 kilometres from HQ, give or take a centimetre.

'Erm, Danger Mouse . . . ?' I said, as white spots began twirling and whirling in front of my eyes.

'That's me!' yelled Danger Mouse, cartwheeling past at speed. 'What do you think of my anti-villain move? It's a bit retro, but I think it makes a nice change

from Mouse Fu and kick-boxing. If I do enough cartwheels, I'm bound to collide with the invisible enemy sooner or later. But enough about me and my cool moves. What's up, Penfold?'

'B-B-B-BLIZZARD!' I stammered, just before giant falling snowflakes started to hit me squarely in the face.

'Hmm,' said Danger Mouse, coming to a halt upside down. 'That's a nuisance. I wonder how we're going to get out of *this* perilous situation . . . ?'

'This way!' called Julian. 'I know this place like the back of my paw!'

'Isn't this brilliant?' said Danger Mouse, a few minutes later.

'I haven't been this comfortable since I last stayed at the Ritz,' I grumbled sarcastically. 'But I suppose it's nice to be out of the sub-zero storm.'

I took a look around Julian's super-top-secret cave. A soft light glowed at the narrow entrance, where a curtain of snow still fell. The walls glistened frostily and the floor was covered with moss. Actually, compared to the blizzard outside, it was almost cosy in here. This was my kind of survival. A sofa, a cup of tea and a crossword and it would be PERFECT. I heaved a deep sigh of relief. At last. A moment of calm. There wasn't a smidge of danger *anywhere*.

FLASH. We all ducked as the cave was

flooded with blue light that crackled and
blaze as it bounced from wall to wall.

'We're under attack!' shouted Danger
Mouse, somersaulting into action.

CHAPTER NINE

Peowwww! Ping! BOOM!
More ferocious flashes lit up the
cave. Blinding blue bolts blazed through
the frosty air, tiny sparkles trailing
behind. Blue lightning crackled to and
fro. It was like a disco gone mad, but I
didn't feel like dancing. If only we could
see whoever was attacking us, we'd be
able to fight back. But we couldn't!

'Penfold, quick!' Danger Mouse said,

dodging a lightning bolt. 'Where's the back door to this cave? You know, the International Safety Standards emergency exit? Because I really hope there's another way out of here. Otherwise . . . we're trapped.'

'Erm, Chief,' I said, 'we're trapped.'

FLASH! It was the biggest blast yet. The ball of blue light careered towards Danger Mouse, scoring a direct hit.

'You're TRAPPED,' squeaked a voice.

'Yes, we've already worked that out, smarty-pants,' said Danger Mouse. Then he raised an eyebrow. 'Hang on . . . who said that?'

'Ha ha ha haaaaaa!'

Whoosh! More balls of sparkling blue light raced through the cave and shot out

of the entrance. '*Catch me if you can, Danger Mouse!*' the invisible enemy cried.

'Cue the *Danger Mouse* theme tune!' said Danger Mouse. He paused. 'Ah. Silly me! We're not on the telly, are we? Hey, I don't suppose there's any chance you could sing it, Penfold . . . ? It makes me feel sort of invincible when I'm about to outwit an evil villain. You know, gives me a bit of a boost.'

'No problem, Chief!' I said.

Danger Mouse stood for a moment in the entrance, silhouetted against the glare of blue light and poised to fight our invisible enemy.

'He's the greatest!
He's fantastic!

Wherever there is danger –'

'Actually, Penfold,' said Danger Mouse, popping his head back into the cave, his fingers in his ears, 'on second thoughts, maybe not?' Then – *peow!* – he was gone.

Ahem. I have always been much better at making tea than singing lead vocals.

'Oh, I don't dare look!' wailed Julian, covering his eyes with his paws. 'What's going on out there?!'

I crept to the entrance of the cave and peered out. The snow was thick and heavy. Everything was brilliant white, except for when blinding flashes turned everything a bright blue. I spied Danger Mouse leaping sideways, as if he were trying to save a goal. The whiteness swallowed him. *Gulp*.

And then – ooh, there he was! I watched
in awe as Danger Mouse dived horizontally
in the other direction . . . Ah. Gone again.

Just as I was wondering exactly how loudly
I would have to shout for Colonel K and
Squawkencluck to hear me, the most peculiar
thing floated past. It was small, with a big
head and tiny arms and legs, and it was made
of pure nothingness. Where snow should have
been falling, there was just a blank. It was as
if someone had rubbed out the snow with a
villain-shaped eraser. And I didn't think the
illustrator had done it.

It wasn't me, guv.

Love,

Penfold's illustrator

Then the explanation popped into my head with a big *PING*.

'Danger Mouse!' I cried, running out of the cave and into the storm. 'Snowflakes can't fall through our invisible enemy, which means the blizzard's making the villain, um, un-invisible. I mean, *visible*! And they're over there!'

'Curse you, Penfold!' hissed the squeaky voice. The see-through shape turned in my direction and pointed an accusing finger. 'Why did you have to blow my cover?'

Yikes. She might be invisible, but that didn't stop this week's villain being INCREDIBLY SCARY.

'Well done, Penfold!' said Danger
Mouse, launching out of the snowstorm
with his very best Mouse Fu kick. 'Wait a
minute . . . I recognize that voice! Ooh, who
is it? Don't tell me. Don't tell me . . .'

'I can't tell you, Chief,' I pointed out. 'I
don't know.'

'Ivana the Invisible!' Danger Mouse
slapped his thigh. 'I should have guessed it
was you – ouch!' He clutched his lower leg.
'You kicked me in the shin!' He jerked to the
left. 'Now you've pinched me!'

'So?' screamed the furious Ivana. 'You
locked me in the Arkwright Asylum for
the Criminally Challenged! Believe me,
Danger Mouse, we're nowhere *near* even.
I will have my revenge! I will outwit you

once and for all!' With that, she swallow-dived back into the cave.

Oh, no . . . If Ivana was inside and out of the storm, that meant the snow wouldn't show where she, um, wasn't. In other words, she would be invisible once more!

'Quick!' cried Danger Mouse, also swallow-diving into the cave. At the last minute, he tucked into a forward roll,

tumbled to a halt and landed on his feet.

I ran back inside after him. There's such a thing as too much swallow-diving, you know.

I skidded to a halt in the middle of the cave and found Danger Mouse looking all about. 'Drat and double drat!' he said. 'Julian's gone! Ivana must have yeti-napped him!'

Oh, no! The world's kindest yeti was in Ivana's evil clutches. We had to rescue him! There was just one thing I didn't understand. 'Er, how can she have done that, Chief?' I said. 'There's only one way out.'

'Let's see about that, Penfold,' said Danger Mouse.

Danger Mouse pulled a match from behind his ear and struck it on the side of the cave. It flared at once, casting a warm, flickering glow over the rocky surface. And there, at the very back of the cave, was the totally obvious thing we'd missed earlier – a heavy wooden door set into the stone wall. A metal arm with a weight kept the door shut. A faint neon sign above it said: EXIT.

'See?' said Danger Mouse, with a broad grin. 'I knew that International Safety Standards would be upheld. Ow! Ow! Ow!'

'What is it?' I cried. 'Is Ivana back?'

'No,' said Danger Mouse. 'The match just burned down to my fingers.' He blew it out and lit another one. 'Come on,

Penfold,' he said. He grabbed the door handle and began to push.

Creeeeeeeak!

Oh, crikey. The door seemed to think it was in a haunted house. Right now, I wished I were in one too. But I followed Danger Mouse and his lit match through the emergency exit into the heavy gloom beyond. The door thudded shut behind us. The tiny flame flickered uneasily in the darkness, revealing a twisty-turny tunnel. And then it went out.

'Ha!' said Danger Mouse. 'Would you believe it? That was my last match!'

'Oh, GREAT,' I said, reaching inside my suit for my very last jar of jam.

'Awww, that's what I love about you,

Penfold,' said Danger Mouse, clapping me on the back. 'You're always so positive.'

A distant blue flash pierced through the pitch-black darkness in front of us.

'That-a-way!' cried Danger Mouse, darting towards it.

I stumbled after him, shovelling strawberry jam into my mouth and *boing*-ing off the rocky walls as I ran. The tunnel bent this way and that. It forked. It did U-turns. There were crossroads. Possibly even a flyover. But always the blue flashes led us after Ivana the Invisible and deep into the mountain . . . until the tunnel opened out into a vast cave hung all around with stalactites.

And there was Julian. He sat on a rock

with his head in his hands. 'Sorry, chaps,'
he said. 'I followed the blue flashes and
then, before I knew it, I was here. Now I
don't know my way out.'

'*Ha ha ha haaaaaa!*'

'Ivana!' said Danger Mouse, his hands on his hips. 'This is not even a tiny bit funny. Now, show us the exit and we'll say no more about it. Come on. Chop-chop.'

Blue sparks exploded on the far side of the cavern. '*Not on your nelly!*' cried Ivana. 'This is exactly where I want you. You're TRAPPED in my secret Himalayan lair, Danger Mouse.

Who do you think will save you now? The yeti that's too polite to say boo to a goose? Or that cowardly sidekick of yours? He couldn't survive in a survival-gear shop!

This mountain is filled with tunnels.
You're never going to find your way out!
Especially after I block the entrance to
this underground labyrinth with the
world's biggest avalanche. I've been
practicing my avalanches, and I'm VERY
good at them.' Ivana let out another nasty
laugh. 'You're finished, Danger Mouse.
FINISHED!'

CHAPTER TEN

'I hate to nitpick, but actually I'm not finished,' said Danger Mouse. 'We're only on page one hundred and thirty-one. Look. There's still loads of time for me to make a brilliant comeback.'

'That's what you think,' said Ivana. 'I'm off to see to that avalanche outside – and don't try and follow my secret route out of these caves . . . BECAUSE I'M INVISIBLE! *Ha ha haaaa, byeeeeeee!*'

'*Sniff! Sniff!*'

I knew exactly how the yeti felt. We were trapped. Ivana had taken so many lefts and rights and round-the-bends on the way here that we'd *never* be able to retrace our steps to the entrance. There were a thousand different routes we could take. And it was dark. At least we'd had the blue flashes to follow on the way here.

'*Sniff! Sniff!*'

'Don't cry, Julian,' said Danger Mouse. 'We'll find our way out.'

'I'm not crying,' said Julian. 'I can smell jam. I love jam.'

'Oops,' I said, swallowing the last jammy strawberry from the pot I'd opened earlier. Oh, dear. It hadn't lasted very long. 'That was my very last pot. I just finished it.'

'But I can still smell it,' said the yeti. He padded around in the darkness, still sniffing. Then there was an enormous, lip-smacking SLURRRP. 'Mmm. Found it. Lovely. Ooh, here's a bit more. Deeeelicious.' He carried on sniffing and slurping contentedly. 'I say, Penfold. You must have dribbled a lot of jam. There are splodges of it all across the floor.'

'Hansel-and-Gretel-tastic!' exclaimed Danger Mouse. 'Penfold, you've laid us a trail. All we have to do is follow it back to the emergency exit from Julian's cave and we'll be able to foil Ivana's wicked plans before she seals us inside the mountain for ever. Come on, Julian. Get sniffing!'

'My pleasure,' said Julian. 'If you'd like to hop on board,' he added, 'I don't mind giving you both a ride. But hang on tight. It's a little-known fact that a yeti set the land-speed record a hundred years ago. It's just that no one from the world records office could find them to record it.'

We jumped on to his back, and then – *wheeeeeee!* We shot through the tunnels like a rocket, zigzagging along dark passages, travelling ever upward as if we were riding the world's craziest rollercoaster. Would we make it? I didn't know! I hadn't read the last page yet! On and on we went, Julian sniffing and slurping like a demon until – *BOOM!*

We burst through the emergency exit and out of the cave into broad daylight.

'Brilliant work, Julian,' said Danger Mouse, leaping off the yeti's back. Julian smiled back at him dreamily, his beard dripping with strawberry jam. 'Penfold, you know what this means, don't you?'

'Yes, we've escaped!' I said, hopping off to stand beside Danger Mouse. 'Now we can go home to HQ for tea!'

'Er, not quite,' said Danger Mouse. 'It means that the entrance is clear, which also means that we've beaten Ivana the Invisible to the exit. Now we can ambush her, take her back to Arkwright Asylum and *then* the job'll be a good 'un!'

'Ah, yes,' I said, waving goodbye in my

mind to the cup of tea I'd been planning to drink at HQ. 'Of course. I forgot about Ivana. So how are we going to capture her, Chief? If we can't see her, I mean.'

'Good question, Penfold,' said Danger Mouse. 'Did we bring absolutely *everything* out of the Mark IV's boot when we left base camp? I don't suppose you happen to have a really useful gadget tucked away in your pocket, do you? It's a long shot, I know, but we could do with a cracking coincidence to finish this book off . . .'

With a shrug, I patted myself down like a customs official. Then I frowned. There *was* something in my pocket. Something soft and squishy. How strange. It didn't feel like a jar of jam.

I reached inside and pulled out the tiny pocket fishing net I'd packed at the very beginning of the adventure. 'What a shame,' I said. 'We could really have done with this before now. Imagine all the fish we could have caught yesterday.'

Danger Mouse's eyes lit up as he took it. 'And imagine all the invisible villains we can catch *today*,' he said. 'Penfold, I don't know what I'd do without you! Now, all we need to do is hold this net over the mouth of the cave and when Ivana appears she'll fall straight into our trap!'

'*Ha ha ha haaaaaa!*' cried Ivana, beside me.

Ah. Maybe not, then.

'Too slow!' she shrieked. 'Did you really think you would capture me with such an obvious plan? You were too busy congratulating yourselves on your brilliant idea to notice me escaping from the cave after you!'

'Oh, bother,' drawled Danger Mouse, casually twirling the fishing net in the air.

'I don't know what you think you're going to do with that,' said Ivana. 'You can't see me, remember? I'm INVISIBLE.'

'Yes, you keep mentioning that you're invisible . . . but your footprints in the snow aren't,' said Danger Mouse.

And he let go of the net. It unfurled in the air and fell quickly back to earth, trapping her beneath it with a *whumph!*

'Gotcha,' he said.

'Oh, no you haven't!' screamed a furious Ivana, lifting something massive and, of course, invisible, on to her shoulder and pointing it straight at Danger Mouse. It was perfectly outlined by the fishing net. Oh, dear. It looked an awful lot like an Invisi-rocket, Ivana's famous weapon.

'RUN, Danger Mouse!' I cried.

In hair-raisingly slow motion, a blue bolt of light leaped from the invisible weapon, just as a blindingly white and exceptionally furry shape dived in front of Danger Mouse. It was Julian. The yeti was trying to protect him!

'Noooooooooo!' I cried.

And then the most astonishing thing happened. The blue flame didn't splat the yeti . . . it bounced right off him. Wow! Julian's fur was so shiny and reflective that it completely deflected Ivana's blazing bolt! Stunned into silence, I watched as the bolt shot straight back towards Ivana and smashed into her. She collapsed in a heap in the sparkling snow and stopped saying '*Ha ha ha haaaaaa!*' at last. (She did manage a small '*drat!*' though, just in case anyone was worried about her.)

'Julian, you're a hero!' said Danger Mouse, bumping knuckles with Julian. 'I never could have dodged that.'

I opened my mouth to object – Danger Mouse could dodge anything! But then

Danger Mouse caught my eye and gave me a wink.

OF COURSE. Julian had always wanted to be a good guy. And now Danger Mouse had given him the chance!

'I never thought I'd say this,' Danger Mouse went on, 'but sometimes, running away extremely quickly and hiding behind a giant Himalayan yeti is actually the smartest way to survive – and to defeat the villain.' He gave me a high five. 'Did you hear that, Penfold? It's not all about bivouacs and knots.'

'Yes, Chief,' I said with a grin. 'Er, Chief?' I added. 'I did find one more thing in my pocket. This.' I held out a small pillar-box-shaped object.

'Excellent!' said Danger Mouse. 'It's the SFTMFN button!'

'Pardon?' I said. 'Is that Martian for 'HOME' or did you get a really bad selection of Scrabble letters?'

Danger Mouse pushed the button. 'It stands for Send For The Mark IV Now, of course,' he said. 'I'm surprised you didn't work it out. Ah, here we are.' The Mark IV zoomed out of the clouds and skidded to a halt beside us, sending up a spray of mud and snow behind it.

Julian's eyes goggled.

'Fancy a lift?' Danger Mouse asked him. 'It's all waiting for you in London, you know. Fame. Fortune. Chicken tikka masala. A plinth at the Natural History Museum.'

'Thanks awfully,' said the yeti, 'but I'm thinking of going to the North Pole on holiday. It's been fun showing the world that I'm a good guy, but it's getting a bit crowded in the Himalayas. Lovely to meet you, though. Take care. Cheers, thanks a lot, ta.' And, after hugging us both tight in a giant yeti hug, he slipped away into the mountains again.

'What about meeee?' whined Ivana. 'Don't leave me tangled in this net. I've got a fear of nets. Hairnets. Net curtains. All of them. Come on, I'll do *anything*. I'll eat Brussels sprouts. I'll even give you my whole store of Invisi-rockets if you'll just let me out.'

'Done!' said Danger Mouse. 'Brussels sprouts it is!'

Ivana's face fell.

'Only joking! Back to the Arkwright Asylum for you!' Danger Mouse laughed, bundling this week's villain into the back of the Mark IV. He turned to me. 'I don't know about you, Penfold, but I'm SO over this survival lark. How about we do an Everest fly-by instead of climbing it?'

'Oh yes, Chief,' I said, reaching into the glove compartment for the teabags that had been there all the time. 'Fancy a spot of high tea on the way? Geddit, Chief? *High* tea?!'

And we laughed all the way over the Himalay-*ha-ha*s.

ACTIVITIES

1. Danger Mouse and Penfold find tons of dangerous stuff in the Himalayas. Can you help them out by identifying some of the really perilous things in this word search?

B	T	S	J	I	D	A	K	E	H
L	P	S	T	G	E	N	H	L	I
I	G	E	E	T	P	C	L	J	A
Z	Y	E	C	R	N	X	Q	D	A
Z	W	S	E	A	E	A	N	W	T
A	P	A	L	V	L	V	Y	K	W
R	Z	A	J	D	S	K	E	J	O
D	V	M	O	U	N	T	A	I	N
A	E	S	S	A	V	E	R	C	S
X	O	Q	Q	F	R	S	K	E	A

AVALANCHE   CREVASSE   MOUNTAIN

BLIZZARD   EVEREST   YETI

2. A gazillion essential items dropped out of the Mark IV on the way from HQ to the Himalayas. But can you remember what they were? Look at the items here and circle the ones we saw falling from the Mark IV on page 15.

3. Did you know that this book contains all the clues you need to work out Danger Mouse's favourite UK seaside resort? (And, yes, we know this has nothing to do with yetis, but aren't you ready for some SUN after all that snow?) Simply search for these letters to spell it out.

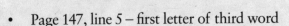

- Page 147, line 5 – first letter of third word
- Page 66, line 1 – first letter of first word
- Page 143, line 2 – second letter of third word
- Page 138, line 3 – third letter of second word
- Page 12, line 2 – second letter of fourth word
- Page 134, line 3 – first letter of first word
- Page 24, line 4 – second letter of first word
- Page 103, line 2 – fourth letter of first word